Bret Harte

The lost Galleon and other Tales

Bret Harte

The lost Galleon and other Tales

ISBN/EAN: 9783337024772

Printed in Europe, USA, Canada, Australia, Japan

Cover: Foto ©Andreas Hilbeck / pixelio.de

More available books at **www.hansebooks.com**

THE

LOST GALLEON

AND

OTHER TALES.

BY

FR. BRET HARTE.

SAN FRANCISCO:
TOWNE & BACON, PRINTERS.
1867.

BEFORE THE CURTAIN.

Behind the footlights hangs the rusty baize;
A trifle shabby in the upturned blaze
Of flaring gas, and curious eyes that gaze.

The stage, methinks, perhaps is none too wide;
And hardly fit for royal Richard's stride,
Or Falstaff's bulk, or Denmark's youthful pride.

Ah well! no passion walks its humble boards—
O'er it no king nor valiant Hector lords—
The simplest skill is all its space affords—

The song and jest, the dance and trifling play—
The local hit at follies of the day—
The trick to pass an idle hour away—

For these, no trumpets that announce the Moor—
No blast that makes the hero's welcome sure—
A single fiddle in the overture!

CONTENTS.

TALES AND LEGENDS.

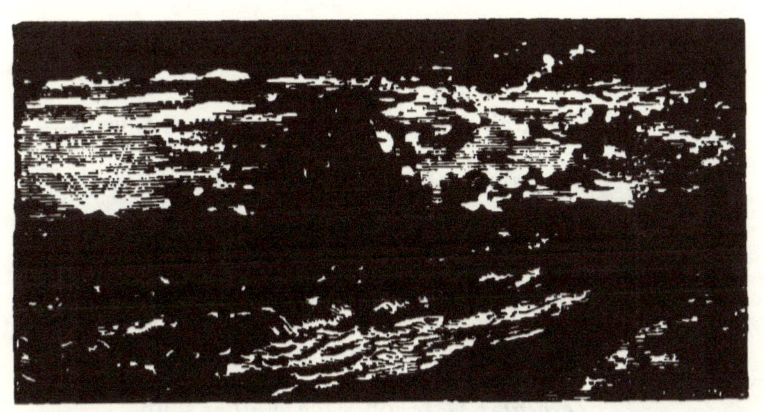

THE LOST GALLEON.

IN sixteen hundred and forty-one,
The regular yearly galleon,
Laden with odorous gums and spice,
India cottons and India rice,
And the richest silks of far Cathay,
Was due at Acapulco Bay.

Due she was and over-due,
Galleon, merchandise and crew,
Creeping along through rain and shine,
Through the tropics, under the Line.

The trains were waiting outside the walls,
The wives of sailors thronged the town,
The traders sat by their empty stalls,
And the viceroy himself came down.
The bells in the tower were all a-trip,
Te deums were on each Father's lip,
The limes were ripening in the sun
For the sick of the coming galleon.

All in vain. Weeks passed away,
And yet no galleon saw the bay.
India goods advanced in price,
The Governor missed his favorite spice,
The Señoritas mourned for sandal,
And the famous cottons of Coromandel.
And some for an absent lover lost,
And one for a husband—Donna Julia,
Wife of the Captain, tempest-tossed,
In circumstances so peculiar—
Even the Fathers, unawares,
Grumbled a little at their prayers,
And all along the coast that year,

Votive candles were scarce and dear.

Never a tear bedims the eye
That time and patience will not dry;
Never a lip is curved with pain
That can't be kissed into smiles again.
And these same truths, as far as I know,
Obtained on the coast of Mexico
More than two hundred years ago,
In sixteen hundred and fifty-one—
Ten years after the deed was done—
And folks had forgotten the galleon.
The divers plunged in the Gulf for pearls,
White as the teeth of the Indian girls;
The traders sat by their full bazaars;
The mules with many a weary load,
And oxen, dragging their creaking cars,
Came and went on the mountain road.

Where was the galleon all this while—
Wrecked on some lonely coral isle?
Burnt by the roving sea marauders,
Or sailing north under secret orders?

Had she found the Anian passage famed,
By lying Moldonado claimed,
And sailed through the sixty-fifth degree
Direct to the North Atlantic sea?
Or had she found the "River of Kings,"
Of which De Fonté told such strange things
In sixteen-forty? Never a sign,
East, or West, or under the Line,
They saw of the missing galleon;
Never a sail, or plank, or chip,
They found of the long-lost treasure ship,
Or enough to build a tale upon.
But when she was lost, and where and how,
Are the facts we're coming to just now.

Take, if you please, the chart of that day,
Published at Madrid—*por el Rey*—
Look for a spot in the old South Sea,
The hundred and eightieth degree
Longitude, west of Madrid: there,
Under the equatorial glare,
Just where the East and West are one,

You 'll find the missing galleon;
You 'll find the *San Gregorio*, yet
Riding the seas, with sails all set,
Fresh as upon the very day
She sailed from Acapulco Bay.

How did she get there? What strange spell
Kept her two hundred years so well,
Free from decay and mortal taint?
What—but the prayers of a patron saint!

A hundred leagues from Manila town,
The *San Gregorio's* helm came down;
Round she went on her heel, and not
A cable's length from a galliot
That rocked on the waters, just abreast
Of the galleon's course, which was west-sou-west.

Then said the galleon's Commandante,
General Pedro Sobriente,
(That was his rank on land and main,
A regular custom of Old Spain:)
"My pilot is dead of scurvy; may

I ask the longitude, time, and day?"
The first two given and compared,
The third—the Commandante stared!
"The *first* of June? I make it second."
Said the stranger, "Then you 've wrongly reckoned;
I make it *first:* as you came this way,
You should have lost—d' ye see—a day—
Lost a day, as you plainly see,
On the hundred and eightieth degree."
"Lost a day?" "Yes, if not rude,
When did you make east longitude?"
"On the ninth of May—our patron's day."
"On the ninth?—*you had no ninth of May!*
Eighth and tenth was there—but stay"—
Too late—for the galleon bore away.

Lost was the day they should have kept,
Lost unheeded and lost unwept;
Lost in a way that made search vain,
Lost in the trackless and boundless main;
Lost like the day of Job's awful curse,
In his third chapter, third and fourth verse:

Wrecked was their patron's only day—
What would the holy fathers say?

Said the Fray Antonio Estavan,
The galleon's chaplain—a learned man—
"Nothing is lost that you can regain:
And the way to look for a thing, is plain
To go where you lost it, back again.
Back with your galleon till you see
The hundred and eightieth degree.
Wait till the rolling year goes round,
And there will the missing day be found.
For you'll find—if computation 's true,
That sailing *East* will give to you
Not only one ninth of May, but *two*—
One for the good saint's present cheer,
And one for the day we lost last year."

Back to the spot sailed the galleon;
Where, for a twelve-month, off and on
The hundred and eightieth degree,
She rose and fell on a tropic sea.

But lo! when it came the ninth of May,
All of a sudden becalmed she lay
One degree from that fatal spot,
Without the power to move a knot;
And of course the moment she lost her way,
Gone was her chance to save that day.

To cut a lengthening story short,
She never saved it. Made the sport
Of evil spirits, and baffling wind,
She was always before or just behind,
One day too soon or one day too late,
And the sun, meanwhile, would never wait.
She had two Eighths, as she idly lay,
Two Tenths, but never a *Ninth* of May.
And there she rides through two hundred years
Of dreary penance and anxious fears:
Yet through the grace of the saint she served,
Captain and crew are still preserved.

By a computation that still holds good,
Made by the Holy Brotherhood,
The *San Gregorio* will cross that line,

In nineteen hundred and thirty-nine :
Just three hundred years to a day
From the time she lost the ninth of May.
And the folk in Acapulco town,
Over the waters, looking down,
Will see in the glow of the setting sun,
The sails of the missing galleon,
And the royal standard of Philip *Rey;*
The gleaming mast and glistening spar,
As she nears the surf of the outer bar.
A *Te Deum* sung on her crowded deck,
An odor of spice along the shore,
A crash, a cry from a shattered wreck—
And the yearly galleon sails no more,
In or out of the olden bay,
For the blessed patron has found his day.

Such is the legend. Hear this truth :
Over the trackless past, somewhere,
Lie the lost days of our tropic youth,

Only regained by faith and prayer,
Only recalled by prayer and plaint :—
Each lost day has its patron saint !

JOHN BURNS OF GETTYSBURG.

HAVE you heard the story that gossips tell
Of Burns of Gettysburg?—No? Ah, well;
Brief is the glory that hero earns,
Briefer the story of poor JOHN BURNS:
He was the fellow who won renown—
The only man who didn't back down
When the rebels rode through his native town;
But held his own in the fight next day,
When all his townsfolk ran away.
That was in July, sixty-three,
The very day that General Lee,
Flower of Southern chivalry,
Baffled and beaten, backward reeled
From a stubborn Meade and a barren field.

I might tell how, but the day before,
JOHN BURNS stood at his cottage door,
Looking down the village street,
Where, in the shade of his peaceful vine,
He heard the low of his gathered kine,
And felt their breath with incense sweet;
Or, I might say, when the sunset burned
The old farm gable, he thought it turned
The milk that fell in a babbling flood
Into the milk-pail, red as blood!
Or, how he fancied the hum of bees
Were bullets buzzing among the trees.
But all such fanciful thoughts as these
Were strange to a practical man like Burns,
Who minded only his own concerns,
Troubled no more by fancies fine
Than one of his calm-eyed, long-tailed kine—
Quite old-fashioned and matter-of-fact,
Slow to argue, but quick to act.
That was the reason, as some folk say,
He fought so well on that terrible day.

And it was terrible: On the right
Raged for hours the heady fight,
Thundered the battery's double bass—
Difficult music for men to face;
While on the left—where now the graves
Undulate like the living waves,
That all that day unceasing swept
Up to the pits the rebels kept—
Round shot ploughed the upland glades,
Sown with bullets, reaped with blades;
Shattered fences here and there
Tossed their splinters in the air;
The very trees were stripped and bare;
The barns that once held yellow grain
Were heaped with harvests of the slain,
The cattle bellowed on the plain,
The turkeys screamed with might and main,
And brooding barn-fowl left their rest
With strange shells bursting in each nest.

Just where the tide of battle turns,
Erect and lonely stood old John Burns.

How do you think the man was dressed?
He wore an ancient long buff vest,
Yellow as saffron—but his best;
And, buttoned over his manly breast,
Was a bright blue coat, with a rolling collar,
And large gilt buttons—size of a dollar—
With tails that the country-folk called "swaller."
He wore a broad-brimmed, bell-crowned hat,
White as the locks on which it sat.
Never had such a sight been seen
For forty years on the village green,
Since old John Burns was a country beau,
And went to the "quiltings" long ago.

Close at his elbows all that day,
Veterans of the Peninsula,
Sunburnt and bearded, charged away;
And striplings, downy of lip and chin—
Clerks that the Home Guard mustered in—
Glanced as they passed at the hat he wore,
Then at the rifle his right hand bore;
And hailed him from out their youthful lore,

With scraps of a slangy *repertoire:*
"How are you, White Hat!" "Put her through!"
"Your head's level," and "Bully for you!"
Called him "Daddy"—begged he'd disclose
The name of the tailor who made his clothes,
And what was the value he set on those;
While Burns, unmindful of jeer and scoff,
Stood there picking the rebels off—
With his long brown rifle, and bell-crown hat,
And the swallow-tails they were laughing at.

'Twas but a moment, for that respect
Which clothes all courage their voices checked;
And something the wildest could understand
Spake in the old man's strong right hand;
And his corded throat, and the lurking frown
Of his eyebrows under his old bell-crown;
Until as they gazed, there crept an awe
Through the ranks in whispers, and some men saw,
In the antique vestments and long white hair,
The Past of the Nation in battle there;
And some of the soldiers since declare

That the gleam of his old white hat afar,
Like the crested plume of the brave Navarre,
That day was their oriflamme of war.

So raged the battle. You know the rest:
How the rebels, beaten and backward pressed,
Broke at the final charge, and ran.
At which John Burns—a practical man—
Shouldered his rifle, unbent his brows,
And then went back to his bees and cows.

That is the story of old John Burns;
This is the moral the reader learns:
In fighting the battle, the question's whether
You'll show a hat that's white, or a feather!

THE TALE OF A PONY.

NAME of my heroine, simply "Rose;"
Surname, tolerable only in prose;
Habitat, Paris—that is where
She resided for change of air;
Ætat xx; complexion fair,
Rich, good-looking, and *débonnair*,
Smarter than Jersey-lightning—There!
That's her photograph—done with care.

In Paris, whatever they do besides—
EVERY LADY IN FULL DRESS, RIDES!
Moire antiques you never meet
Sweeping the filth of a dirty street;

But every woman's claim to *ton*
Depends upon
The team she drives, whether phaeton,
Landeau, or britzka. Hence it 's plain
That Rose, who was of her toilette vain,
Should have a team that ought to be
Equal to any in all *Paris!*

"Bring forth the horse!"—the *commissaire*
Bowed, and brought Miss Rose a pair
Leading an equipage rich and rare:
"Why doth that lovely lady stare?"
Why? The tail of the off gray mare
Is bobbed—by all that 's good and fair!
Like the shaving brushes that soldiers wear,
Scarcely showing as much back-hair
As Tam O'Shanter's "Meg,"—and there
Lord knows she 'd little enough to spare.

That stare and frown the Frenchman knew,
But did—as well-bred Frenchmen do:
Raised his shoulders above his crown,
Joined his thumbs, with the fingers down,

And said, "Ah, Heaven!"—then, "Mademoiselle,
Delay one minute, and all is well!"
He went; returned; by what good chance
These things are managed so well in France
I cannot say—but he made the sale,
And the bob-tailed mare had a flowing tail.

All that is false in this world below
Betrays itself in a love of show;
Indignant Nature hides her lash
In the purple-black of a dyed moustache;
The shallowest fop will trip in French,
The would-be critic will misquote Trench;
In short, you're always sure to detect
A sham in the things folks most affect;
Bean-pods are noisiest when dry,
And you always wink with your weakest eye:
And that's the reason the old gray mare
Forever had her tail in the air,
With flourishes beyond compare—
    Though every whisk
    Incurred the risk

Of leaving that sensitive region bare—
She did some things that you could n't but feel
She would n't have done had her tail been real.

Champs Elysées: Time, past five;
There go the carriages—look alive!
Everything that man can drive,
Or his inventive skill contrive—
Yankee buggy or English "chay;"
Dog-cart, droschky, and smart coupé,
A *desobligeante* quite bulky,
(French idea of a Yankee *sulky*;)
Band in the distance, playing a march,
Footmen standing stiff as starch;
Savans, lorettes, deputies, Arch-
Bishops, and there together range
Sous-lieutenants and *cent*-gardes—(strange
Way these soldier-chaps make change)—
Mixed with black-eyed Polish dames,
With unpronounceable awful names;
Laces tremble, and ribbons flout,
Coachmen wrangle and gend'armes shout—

Tale of a Pony.

Bless us! what is the row about?
Ah! here comes Rosey's new turn-out!

Smart! You bet your life, 'twas that!
Nifty! (short for *magnificat*)
Mulberry panels—heraldic spread—
Ebony wheels picked out with red,
And two gray mares that were thoroughbred;
No wonder that every dandy's head
Was turned by the turn-out—and 'twas said
That Caskowhisky, (friend of the Czar)
A very good *whip*, (as Russians are)
Was tied to Rosey's triumphal car,
Entranced, the reader will understand,
By "ribbons" that graced her head and hand.

Alas! the hour you think would crown
Your highest wishes, should let you down!
Or Fate should turn, by your own mischance,
Your victor's car to an ambulance;
From cloudless heavens her lightnings glance,
(And these things happen, even in France;)
And so Miss Rose, as she trotted by—

The cynosure of every eye—
Saw to her horror the off-mare shy—
Flourish her tail so exceeding high
That, disregarding the closest tie,
And without giving a reason why,
She flung that tail so free and frisky,
Off in the face of Ca-kowhisky!

Excuses, blushes, smiles: in fine,
End of the pony's tail, and mine!

THE MIRACLE OF PADRE JUNIPERO.

THIS is the tale that the Chronicle
Tells of the wonderful miracle
Wrought by the pious Padre Serro,
The very reverend Junipero.

The Heathen stood on his ancient mound,
Looking over the desert bound
Into the distant, hazy south,
Over the dusty and broad champaign
Where—with many a gaping mouth,
And fissure cracked by the fervid drouth—
For seven months had the wasted plain
Known no moisture of dew or rain.
The wells were empty and choked with sand;
The rivers had perished from the land;

Only the sea fogs, to and fro,
Slipped like ghosts of the streams below.
Deep in its bed lay the river's bones,
Bleaching in pebbles and milk-white stones,
And tracked o'er the desert faint and far,
Its ribs shone bright on each sandy bar.

Thus they stood, as the sun went down
Over the foot-hills bare and brown;
Thus they looked to the South—wherefrom
The pale-face medicine man should come.
Not in anger, or in strife,
But to bring—so ran the tale—
The welcome springs of eternal life,
The living waters that should not fail.

Said one: "He will come like Manitou,
Unseen, unheard, in the falling dew."
Said another: "He will come full soon
Out of the round-faced watery moon."
And another said: "He is here!" and lo—
Faltering, staggering, feeble and slow—
Out from the desert's blinding heat
The Padre dropped at the heathens' feet

They stood and gazed for a little space
Down on his pallid and care-worn face,
And a smile of scorn went round the band
As they touched alternate with foot and hand
This mortal waif, that the outer space
Of dim mysterious sky and sand
Flung with so little of Christian grace
Down on their barren, sterile strand.

Said one to him : " It seems thy god
Is a very pitiful kind of god ;
He could not shield thine aching eyes
From the blowing desert sands that rise,
Nor turn aside from thy old gray head
The glittering blade that is brandishéd
By the sun he set in the heavens high.
He could not moisten thy lips when dry ;
The desert fire is in thy brain ;
Thy limbs are racked with the fever-pain :
If this be the grace he sheweth thee
Who art his servant, what may we,

Strange to his ways and his commands,
Seek at his unforgiving hands?"

"Drink but this cup," said the Padre, straight,
"And thou shalt know whose mercy bore
These aching limbs to your heathen door,
And purged my soul of its gross estate.
Drink in His name, and thou shalt see
The hidden depths of this mystery.
Drink!" and he held the cup. One blow
From the heathen dashed to the ground below
The sacred cup that the Padre bore;
And the thirsty soil drank the precious store
Of sacramental and holy wine,
That emblem and consecrated sign
And blessed symbol of blood divine.

Then, says the legend—(and they who doubt
The same as heretics be accurst)—
From the dry and feverish soil leaped out
A living fountain; a well-spring burst
Over the dusty and broad champaign,
Over the sandy and sterile plain,

Till the granite ribs and the milk-white stones
That lay in the valley—the scattered bones—
Moved in the river and lived again!

Such was the wonderful miracle
Wrought by the cup of wine that fell
From the hands of the pious Padre Serro,
The very reverend Junipero.

NATIONAL AND SANITARY.

The long, long night of Storm and Strife is past;
Alike the grasses spring o'er friend and foe;
And thou, brave heart, whose voice outrode the blast—
Whose kindling thought made every beacon glow—
O friend, who would'st my future work forecast
Pointing this idle pen to higher things—
In these poor songs to thee I still cling fast;
I read, and lo, thy clarion voice still rings
And in mine own refrain, it is thy thought that sings.

THE REVEILLE.

HARK! I hear the tramp of thousands,
And of arméd men the hum;
Lo! a nation's hosts have gathered
Round the quick alarming drum—
Saying, "Come,
Freemen, come!
Ere your heritage be wasted," said the quick alarming drum.

"Let me of my heart take counsel:
War is not of Life the sum;
Who shall stay and reap the harvest
When the autumn days shall come?"
But the drum
Echoed, "Come!
Death shall reap the braver harvest," said the solemn-sounding drum.

"But when won the coming battle,
What of profit springs therefrom?
What if conquest—subjugation—
Even greater ills become?"
But the drum
Answered, "Come!
You must do the sum to prove it," said the Yankee-answering drum.

"What if, 'mid the cannons' thunder,
Whistling shot and bursting bomb—
When my brothers fall around me,
Should my heart grow cold and numb?"
But the drum
Answered, "Come!
Better there in death united, than in life a recreant—Come!"

Thus they answered—hoping, fearing,
Some in faith, and doubting some,
'Till a trumpet-voice proclaiming,
Said, "My chosen people, come!"
Then the drum,
Lo! was dumb,
For the great heart of the nation, throbbing, answered, "Lord, we come!"

OUR PRIVILEGE.

NOT ours, where battle smoke upcurls,
And battle dews lie wet,
To meet the charge that treason hurls
By sword and bayonet.

Not ours to guide the fatal scythe
The fleshless reaper wields;
The harvest moon looks calmly down
Upon our peaceful fields.

The long grass dimples on the hill,
The pines sing by the sea,
And Plenty, from her golden horn,
Is pouring far and free.

O brothers by the further sea,
Think still our faith is warm;
The same bright flag above us waves
That swathed our baby form.

The same red blood that dyes your fields
Here throbs in patriot pride;
The blood that flowed when Lander fell,
And Baker's crimson tide.

And thus apart our hearts keep time
With every pulse ye feel,
And Mercy's ringing gold shall chime
With Valor's clashing steel.

A SECOND REVIEW OF THE GRAND ARMY.

I READ last night of the Grand Review
In Washington's chiefest avenue—
Two Hundred Thousand men in blue
        I think they said was the number—
Till I seemed to hear their trampling feet,
The bugle blast and the drum's quick beat,
The clatter of hoofs in the stony street,
The cheers of people who came to greet,
And the thousand details that to repeat
        Would only my verse encumber—
Till I fell in a reverie, sad and sweet,
        And then to a fitful slumber.

When, lo! in a vision I seemed to stand
In the lonely Capitol. On each hand
Far stretched the portico, dim and grand
Its columns ranged like a martial band
Of sheeted spectres, whom some command
Had called to a last reviewing;
And the streets of the city were white and bare,
No footfall echoed across the square,
But out of the misty midnight air
I heard in the distance a trumpet blare,
And the wandering night-winds seemed to bear
The sound of a far tattooing.

Then I held my breath with fear and dread,
For into the square, with a brazen tread,
There rode a figure whose stately head
O'erlooked the review that morning,
That never bowed from its firm-set seat
When the living column passed its feet,
Yet now rode steadily up the street
To the phantom bugle's warning;

Till it reached the Capitol square, and wheeled,
And there in the moonlight stood revealed
A well-known form that in State and field
Had led our patriot sires;
Whose face was turned to the sleeping camp,
Afar through the river's fog and damp
That showed no flicker, nor waning lamp,
Nor wasted bivouac fires.

And I saw a phantom army come,
With never a sound of fife or drum,
But keeping time to a throbbing hum
Of wailing and lamentation;
The martyred heroes of Malvern Hill,
Of Gettysburg and Chancellorsville,
The men whose wasted figures fill
The patriot graves of the nation.

And there came the nameless dead—the men
Who perished in fever swamp and fen,
The slowly-starved of the prison-pen;
And, marching beside the others,
Came the dusky martyrs of Pillow's fight,

With limbs enfranchised and bearing bright;
I thought—perhaps 'twas the pale moonlight—
They looked as white as their brothers!

And so all night marched the Nation's dead
With never a banner above them spread,
Nor a badge, nor a motto brandishéd;
No mark—save the bare uncovered head
Of the silent bronze Reviewer—
With never an arch save the vaulted sky,
With never a flower save those that lie
On the distant graves—for love could buy
No gift that was purer or truer.

So all night long swept the strange array,
So all night long till the morning gray
I watched for one who had passed away,
With a reverent awe and wonder—
Till a blue cap waved in the length'ning line,
And I knew that one who was kin of mine
Had come, and I spake—and lo! that sign
Awakened me from my slumber.

ON A PEN OF THOMAS STARR KING.

THIS is the reed the dead musician dropped,
With tuneful magic in its sheath still hidden;
The prompt allegro of its music stopped,
Its melodies, unbidden.

But who shall finish the unfinished strain,
Or wake the instrument to awe and wonder,
And bid the slender barrel breathe again—
An organ-pipe of thunder?

His pen! what humbler memories cling about
Its golden curves; what shapes and laughing graces
Slipped from its point when his full heart went out
In smiles and courtly phrases.

The truth half-jesting, half in earnest flung—
The word of cheer, with recognition in it;
The note of alms, whose golden speech outrung
The golden gift within it.

But all in vain the enchanter's wand we wave;
No stroke of ours recalls his magic vision;
The incantation that its power gave
Sleeps with the dead magician.

THE RABBIT OF MALVERN HILLS.

A STORY FOR CHILDREN.

BUNNY, squatting in the grass,
Saw the glancing column pass—
Saw the stripèd banner fly,
And the sabres twinkle by;
Saw the chargers fret and fume,
And the flapping hat and plume—
Saw them with his moist and shy
Most unspeculative eye,
Thinking only in the dew,
That it was a fine review.

'Till a flash—not all of steel—
Where the flying squadrons wheel,
Brought a rumble and a roar
Rolling down the velvet floor,
And like blows of Autumn flail,
Sharply beat the iron hail.

Bunny, thrilled by unknown fears,
Raised his long and pointed ears,
Mumbled his prehensile lip,
Quivered his pulsating hip
When the sharp vindictive yell
Rose above the screaming shell;
Thought the world and all the men—
All the charging squadrons meant—
All were rabbit hunters then,
All to capture him intent.
Bunny was not much to blame,
Wiser folk have thought the same;
Wiser folk, because they spy
Every ill begins with "I."

Wildly panting here and there,

Bunny sought the freer air
From the columns closing in,
From the strange, confusing din;
Till he hopped below the hill,
And saw lying close and still,
Men with muskets in their hands;
Never Bunny understands
That hypocrisy of sleep
In the vigils grim they keep,
As recumbent on that spot,
They elude the level shot.

One, a grave and wearied man,
Thinking of his wife and child
Far beyond the Rapidan,
By the Androscoggin wild,
Felt the little rabbit creep,
Nestling by his arm and side.
Wakened from strategic sleep
To that soft appeal replied;
Drew him to his blackened breast,
And—but you have guessed the rest.

Softly o'er that chosen pair
Omnipresent Love and Carc
Drew a mightier hand and arm,
Shielding each from every harm—
Right and left the bullets waved,
Saved the savior for the saved.

Who believes that equal grace
God extends in every place,
Little difference he scans
'Twixt the rabbit's God, and man's.

OF ONE WHO FELL IN BATTLE.

BY smoke-encumbered field and tangled lane,
Down roads whose dust was laid with scarlet dew,
Past guns dismounted, ragged heaps of slain,
Dark moving files, and bright blades glancing through,
All day the waves of battle swept the plain
Up to the ramparts, where they broke and cast
Thy young life quivering down, like foam before the blast.

Then sank the tumult. Like an angel's wing,
Soft fingers swept thy pulses. The west wind
Whispered fond voices, mingling with the ring
Of Sabbath bells of Peace—such peace as brave men find,
And only look for till the months shall bring
Surcease of Wrong, and fail from out the land
Bondage and shame, and Freedom's altars stand.

THE GODDESS.

"WHO comes?"—the sentry's warning cry,
Rings sharply on the evening air.
Who comes? the challenge—no reply?
Yet something motions there!

A woman, by those graceful folds;
A soldier, by that martial tread.
"Advance three paces. Halt! until
Thy name and rank be said."

"My name?—her name, in ancient song,
Who fearless frcm Olympus came.
Look on me! Mortals know me best
In battle and in flame!"

"Enough! I know that clarion voice;
  I know that gleaming eye and helm—
Those crimson lips—their dew that blends
  The best blood of the realm.

"The young, the brave, the good and wise,
  Have fallen in thy curst embrace.
The juices of the grapes of wrath
  Still stain thy guilty face.

"My brother lies in yonder field,
  Face downward to the quiet grass.
Go back! he cannot see thee now;
  But here thou shalt not pass."

A crack upon the evening air,
  A wakened echo from the hill;
The watch-dog on the distant shore
  Gives mouth—and all is still.

The sentry with his brother lies
  Face downward on the quiet grass,
And by him, in the pale moonshine,
  A shadow seems to pass.

No lance or warlike shield it bears;
  A helmet in its pitying hands
Brings water from the nearest brook,
  To meet his last demands.

Can this be she of haughty mien—
  The Goddess of the Sword and Shield?
Ah, yes! The Grecian poet's myth
  Sways still each battle-field.

For not alone that rugged War
  Some grace or charm from Beauty gains,
But when the Goddess' work is done,
  The Woman's still remains.

"HOW ARE YOU, SANITARY?"

DOWN the picket-guarded lane,
Rolled the comfort-laden wain,
Cheered by shouts that shook the plain,
Soldier-like and merry:
Phrases such as camps may teach,
Sabre cuts of Saxon speech,
Such as "Bully!" "Them's the peach!"
"Wade in, Sanitary!"

Right and left the caissons drew,
As the car went lumbering through,
Quick succeeding in review
Squadrons military;

6*

Sunburnt men, with beards like frieze,
Smooth-faced boys, and cries like these—
"U. S. San. Com." "That's the cheese!"
"Pass in, Sanitary!"

In such cheer it struggled on
Till the battle front was won,
Then the car, its journey done,
Lo, was stationary;
And where bullets whistling fly,
Came the sadder, fainter cry,
"Help us, brothers, ere we die—
Save us, Sanitary!"

Such the work. The phantom flies,
Wrapped in battle-clouds that rise;
But the brave—whose dying eyes,
Veiled and visionary,
See the jasper gates swung wide,
See the parted throng outside—
Hears the voice to those who ride:
"Pass in, Sanitary!"

RELIEVING GUARD—MARCH 4TH, 1864.

CAME the Relief. "What, Sentry, ho!
How passed the night through thy long waking!"
"Cold, cheerless, dark—as may befit
The hour before the dawn is breaking."

"No sight? no sound?" "No; nothing save
The plover from the marshes calling;
And in yon Western sky, about
An hour ago, a Star was falling."

"A star? There's nothing strange in that."
"No, nothing; but, above the thicket,
Somehow it seemed to me that God
Somewhere had just relieved a picket.

A SANITARY MESSAGE.

LAST night, above the whistling wind,
  I heard the welcome rain;
A fusilade upon the roof,
  A tattoo on the pane.
The key-hole piped; the chimney-top
  A warlike trumpet blew,
Yet mingling with these sounds of strife
  A softer voice stole through.

"Give thanks, O brothers," said the voice,
  "That He who sent the rains
Hath spared your fields the scarlet dew
  That drips from patriot veins.

I've seen the grass on Eastern graves
In brighter verdure rise;
But oh, the rain that gave it life
Sprang first from human eyes.

"I come to wash away no stain
Upon your wasted lea;
I raise no banners, save the ones
The forest wave to me.
Upon the mountain side, where Spring
Her farthest picket sets
My reveillé awakes a host
Of grassy bayonets.

"I visit every humble roof;
I mingle with the low;
Only upon the highest peaks
My blessings fall in snow,
Until in tricklings of the stream,
And drainings of the lea,
My unspent bounty comes at last
To mingle with the sea."

And thus, all night above the wind
  I heard the welcome rain;
A fusilade upon the roof,
  A tattoo on the pane.
The key-hole piped; the chimney-top
  A warlike trumpet blew;
But mingling with these sounds of strife
  This hymn of Peace stole through.

MISCELLANEOUS.

TO THE PLIOCENE SKULL.

A GEOLOGICAL ADDRESS.

"SPEAK, O man, less recent! Fragmentary fossil!
Primal pioneer of pliocene formation,
Hid in lowest drifts below the earliest stratum
Of volcanic tufa!

Older than the beasts, the oldest Palæotherium;
Older than the trees, the oldest Cryptogamia;
Older than the hills, those infantile eruptions
Of earth's epidermis!

Eo—Mio—Plio—whatsoe'er the "cene" was
That those vacant sockets filled with awe and wonder—

Whether shores Devonian or Silurian beaches—
Tell us thy strange story!

Or has the professor slightly antedated
By some thousand years thy advent on this planet,
Giving thee an air that's somewhat better fitted
For cold-blooded creatures?

Wert thou true spectator of that mighty forest
When above thy head the stately Sigillaria
Reared its columned trunks in that remote and distant
Carboniferous epoch?

Tell us of that scene—the dim and watery woodland
Songless, silent, hushed, with never bird or insect
Veiled with spreading fronds and screened with tall club-mosses,
Lycopodiacea—

When beside thee walked the solemn Plesiosaurus,
And around thee crept the festive Ichthyosaurus,
While from time to time above thee flew and circled
Cheerful Pterodactyls.

Tell us of thy food—those half marine refections,
Crinoids on the shell and Brachipods *au naturel*—
Cuttle-fish to which the *pieuvre* of Victor Hugo
Seems a periwinkle.

Speak, thou awful vestige of the Earth's creation—
Solitary fragment of remains organic!
Tell the wondrous secret of thy past existence—
Speak! thou oldest primate!"

Even as I gazed, a thrill of the maxilla,
And a lateral movement of the condyloid process,
With post-pliocene sounds of healthy mastication,
Ground the teeth together.

And, from that imperfect dental exhibition,
Stained with expressed juices of the weed Nicotian,
Came these hollow accents, blent with softer murmurs
Of expectoration;

"Which my name is Bowers, and my crust was busted
Falling down a shaft in Calaveras county,
But I'd take it kindly if you'd send the pieces
Home to old Missouri!"

AN ARCTIC VISION.

WHERE the short-legged Esquimaux
Waddle in the ice and snow,
And the playful polar bear
Nips the hunter unaware;
Where by day they track the ermine,
And by night another vermin—
Segment of the frigid zone,
Where the temperature alone
Warms on St. Elias' cone;
Polar dock, where Nature slips
From the ways her icy ships;
Land of fox, and deer, and sable,
Shore end of our western cable—
Let the news that flying goes
Thrill through all your Arctic floes,

And reverberate the boast
From the cliffs of Beechey's coast,
Till the tidings, circling round
Every bay of Norton Sound,
Throw the vocal tide-wave back
To the isles of Kodiac.
Let the stately polar bears
Waltz around the pole in pairs,
And the walrus, in his glee,
Bare his tusk of ivory;
While the bold sea unicorn
Calmly takes an extra horn;
All ye polar skies, reveal your
Very rarest of parhelia;
Trip it, all ye merry dancers,
In the airiest of lancers;
Slide, ye solemn glaciers, slide,
One inch further to the tide.
Nor in rash precipitation
Upset Tyndall's calculation.
Know you not what fate awaits you,
Or to whom the future mates you?

All ye icebergs make salaam—
You belong to Uncle Sam!

On the spot where Eugene Sue
Led his wretched Wandering Jew,
Stands a form whose features strike
Russ and Esquimaux alike.
He it is whom Skalds of old
In their Runic rhymes foretold;
Lean of flank and lank of jaw,
See the real Northern Thor!
See the awful Yankee leering
Just across the Straits of Behring;
On the drifted snow, too plain,
Sinks his fresh tobacco stain
Just beside the deep iden-
Tation of his Number 10.

Leaning on his icy hammer
Stands the hero of this drama,
And above the wild duck's clamor,
In his own peculiar grammar,
With its linguistic disguises,
Lo, the Arctic prologue rises:

"Wa'll, I reckon 'tain't so bad,
Seein' ez 't was all they had;
True, the Springs are rather late
And early Falls predominate;
But the ice crop's pretty sure,
And the air is kind o' pure;
'Taint so very mean a trade,
When the land is all surveyed.
There's a right smart chance for fur-chase
All along this recent purchase,
And unless the stories fail,
Every fish from cod to whale;
Rocks, too; mebbee quartz; let's see—
'T would be strange if there should be—
Seems I've heerd such stories told;
Eh!—why, bless us—yes, it's gold!"

While the blows are falling thick
From his California pick,
You may recognize the Thor
Of the vision that I saw—
Freed from legendary glamour,
See the real magician's hammer.

THE AGED STRANGER.

AN INCIDENT OF THE WAR.

"I WAS with Grant"—the stranger said;
Said the farmer: "Say no more,
But rest thee here at my cottage porch,
For thy feet are weary and sore."

"I was with Grant"—the stranger said;
Said the farmer: "Nay, no more—
I prithee sit at my frugal board,
And eat of my humble store.

"How fares my boy—my soldier boy,
Of the old Ninth Army Corps?—
I warrant he bore him gallantly
In the smoke and the battle's roar!"

"I know him not," said the aged man,
  "And, as I remarked before,
I was with Grant"—"Nay, nay, I know,"
  Said the farmer, "Say no more;

"He fell in battle—I see, alas!
  Thou'dst smooth these tidings o'er--
Nay: speak the truth, whatever it be
  Though it rend my bosom's core.

"How fell he—with his face to the foe,
  Upholding the flag he bore?
O! say not that my boy disgraced
  The uniform that he wore!

"I cannot tell," said the aged man,
  "And should have remarked, before,
That I was with Grant—in Illinois—
  Some three years before the war."

Then the farmer spake him never a word,
  But beat with his fist full sore
That aged man, who had worked for Grant
  Some three years before the war.

THE HERO OF SUGAR PINE.

"OH tell me, Sergeant of Battery B,
Oh, hero of Sugar Pine!
Some glorious deed of the battle field,
Some wonderful feat of thine.

"Some skilful move, when the fearful game
Of battle and life was played
On yon grimy field, whose broken squares
In scarlet and black are laid."

"Ah, stranger, here at my gun all day,
I fought till my final round

Was spent, and I had but powder left,
  And never a shot to be found;

"So I trained my gun on a rebel piece:
  So true was my range and aim,
A shot from his cannon entered mine
  And finished the load of the same!"

"Enough! Oh, Sergeant of Battery B,
  Oh, hero of Sugar Pine!
Alas! I fear that thy cannon's throat
  Can swallow much more than mine!"

THE LEGENDS OF THE RHINE.

BEETLING walls with ivy grown,
Frowning heights of mossy stone—
Turret, with its flaunting flag
Flung from battlemented crag;
Dungeon-keep and fortalice
Looking down a precipice
O'er the darkly glancing wave
By the Lurlie-haunted cave;
Robber haunt and maiden bower
Home of Love, and Crime, and Power—
That's the scenery, in fine,
Of the Legends of the Rhine.

One bold Baron, double-dyed,
Bigamist and Parricide
And, as most the stories run,
Partner of the Evil One;
Injured innocence in white—
Fair, but idiotic quite—
Wringing of her lily hands;
Valor fresh from Paynim lands.
Abbot ruddy, hermit pale
Minstrel, fraught with many a tale,
Are the actors that combine
In the Legends of the Rhine.

Bell-mouthed flagons round a board,
Suits of armor, shield and sword,
Kerchief with its bloody stain,
Ghosts of the untimely slain,
Thunderclap and clanking chain,
Headsman's block and shining axe,
Thumbscrews, crucifixes, racks,
Midnight-tolling chapel bell
Heard across the gloomy fell.

These and other pleasant facts,
Are the properties that shine
In the Legends of the Rhine.

Maledictions, whispered vows,
Underneath the linden boughs;
Murder, Bigamy and Theft,
Travelers of goods bereft,
Rapine, Pillage, Arson, Spoil—
Everything but honest toil,
Are the deeds that best define
Every Legend of the Rhine:

That Virtue always meets reward,
But quicker, when it wears a sword;
That Providence has special care
Of gallant knight and lady fair;
That villians, as a thing of course
Are always haunted by remorse—
Is the moral I opine,
Of the Legends of the Rhine.

THE TWO SHIPS.

AS I stand by the cross on the lone mountain's crest,
Looking over the ultimate sea,
In the gloom of the mountain a ship lies at rest,
And one sails away from the lea;
One spreads its white wings on a far-reaching track,
With pennant and sheet flowing free;
One hides in the shadow with sails laid aback—
The ship that is waiting for me!

But lo, in the distance the clouds break away,
The Gate's glowing portals I see,
And I hear from the outgoing ship in the bay
The song of the sailors in glee;

So I think of the luminous footprints that bore
The comfort o'er dark Galilee,
And wait for the signal to go to the shore
To the ship that is waiting for me.

THE LOST TAILS OF MILETUS.

HIGH on the Thracian hills, half hid in the billows of clover,
Thyme, and the asphodel blooms, and lulled by Pactolian streamlet,
She of Miletus lay, and beside her an aged satyr
Scratched his ear with his hoof, and playfully mumbled his chestnuts.

Vainly the Mænid and the Bassarid gamboled about her,
The free-eyed Bacchante sang, and Pan—the renowned, the accomplished—
Executed his difficult solo. In vain were their gambols and dances:

High o'er the Thracian hills rose the voice of the shepherdess,
wailing.

"Ai! for the fleecy flocks—the meek-nosed, the passionless
faces;
Ai! for the tallow-scented, the straight-tailed, the high-
stepping;
Ai! for the timid glance, which is that which the rustic,
sagacious,
Applies to him who loves but may not declare his passion!"

Her then Zeus answered slow: "O! daughter of song and
sorrow—
Hapless tender of sheep—arise from thy long lamentation.
Since thou canst not trust fate, nor behave as becomes a
Greek maiden,
Look and behold thy sheep."—And lo! they returned to
her tailless!

A GEOLOGICAL MADRIGAL.

AFTER HERRICK.

I HAVE found out a gift for my fair;
I know where the fossils abound,
Where the foot-prints of *Aves* declare
The birds that once walked on the ground;
O, come, and—in technical speech—
We'll walk this Devonian shore,
Or on some Silurian beach
We'll wander, my love, evermore.

I will show thee the sinuous track
By the slow-moving annelid made,
Or the Trilobite that, further back,
In the old Potsdam sandstone was laid.

Thou shalt see, in his Jurassic tomb,
  The Plesiosauras embalmed;
In his Oolitic prime and his bloom—
  Iguanodon safe and unharmed!

You wished—I remember it well,
  And I loved you the more for that wish—
For a perfect cystedian shell
  And a *whole* holocephalic fish.
And O, if Earth's strata contains
  In its lowest Silurian drift,
Or Palæozoic remains
  The same—'tis your lover's free gift.

Then come, love, and never say nay,
  But calm all your maidenly fears,
We'll note, love, in one summer's day
  The record of millions of years;
And though the Darwinian plan
  Your sensitive feelings may shock,
We'll find the beginning of man—
  Our fossil ancestors in rock!

THE BALLAD OF THE EMEU.

O SAY, have you seen at the Willows so green—
So charming and rurally true—
A singular bird, with a manner absurd,
Which they call the Australian Emeu?
Have you
Ever seen this Australian Emeu?

It trots all around with its head on the ground,
Or erects it quite out of your view;
And the ladies all cry, when its figure they spy,
O! what a sweet, pretty Emeu!
O! do
Just look at that lovely Emeu!

One day to this spot, when the weather was hot,
Came Matilda Hortense Fortescue;
And beside her there came a youth of high name—
Augustus Florell Montague:
The two
Both loved that wild, foreign Emeu.

With two loaves of bread then they fed it, instead
Of the flesh of the white cockatoo,
Which once was its food in that wild neighborhood
Where ranges the sweet Kangaroo;
That too
Is game for the famous Emeu!

Old saws and gimlets but its appetite whets
Like the world-famous bark of Peru;
There's nothing so hard that the bird will discard,
And nothing its taste will eschew
That you
Can give that long-legged Emeu!

The time slipped away, in this innocent play,
When up jumped the bold Montague:

"Where's that specimen pin that I gaily did win
In raffle, and gave unto you,
Fortescue?"
No word spoke the guilty Emeu!

"Quick! tell me his name whom thou gavest that
same,
Ere these hands in thy blood I imbrue!"
"Nay, dearest," she cried, as she clung to his side,
"I'm innocent as that Emeu!"
"Adieu!"
He replied, "Miss M. H. Fortescue!"

Down she dropped at his feet, all as white as a sheet,
As wildly he fled from her view;
He thought 'twas her sin—for he knew not the pin
Had been gobbled up by the Emeu;
All through
The voracity of that Emeu!

THE WILLOWS.

AFTER EDGAR A. POE.

THE skies they were ashen and sober,
  The streets they were dirty and drear;
It was night in the month of October,
  Of my most immemorial year;
Like the skies I was perfectly sober,
  As I stopped at the mansion of Shear—
At the Nightingale—perfectly sober,
  And the willowy woodland, down here.

Here, once in an alley Titanic
  Of Ten-pins—I roamed with my soul—
  Of Ten-pins—with Mary, my soul;
They were days when my heart was volcanic,

And impelled me to frequently roll,
And made me resistlessly roll,
Till my ten-strikes created a panic
In the realms of the Boreal pole,
Till my ten-strikes created a panic,
With the monkey a-top of his pole.

I repeat, I was perfectly sober,
But my thoughts they were palsied and sere—
My thoughts were decidedly queer;
For I knew not the month was October,
And I marked not the night of the year;
I forgot that sweet *morceau* of Auber,
That the band oft performéd down here,
And I mixed the sweet music of Auber
With the Nightingale's music by Shear.

And now as the night was senescent,
And star-dials pointed to morn,
And car-drivers hinted of morn,
At the end of the path a liquescent
And bibulous lustre was born;
'Twas made by the bar-keeper present,

Who mixéd a duplicate horn—
His two hands describing a crescent
Distinct with a duplicate horn.

And I said: "This looks perfectly regal,
For it 's warm, and I know I feel dry—
I am confident that I feel dry:
We have come past the emeu and eagle,
And watched the gay monkey on high:
Let us drink to the emeu and eagle—
To the swan and the monkey on high—
To the eagle and monkey on high;
For this bar-keeper will not inveigle—
Bully boy with the vitreous eye;
He surely would never inveigle—
Sweet youth with the crystalline eye."

But Mary, uplifting her finger,
Said: "Sadly this bar I mistrust—
I fear that this bar does not trust.
Oh, hasten, oh, let us not linger!
Oh, fly—let us fly—ere we must!"
In terror she cried, letting sink her

  Parasol till it trailed in the dust—
In agony sobbed, letting sink her
  Parasol till it trailed in the dust—
  Till it sorrowfully trailed in the dust.

Then I pacified Mary and kissed her,
  And tempted her into the room,
  And conquered her scruples and gloom;
And we passed to the end of the vista,
  But were stopped by the warning of doom—
  By some words that were warning of doom.
And I said: "What is written, sweet sister,
  At the opposite end of the room?"
She sobbed, as she answered, "All liquors
  Must be paid for ere leaving the room."

Then my heart it grew ashen and sober,
  As the streets were deserted and drear—
  For my pockets were empty and drear;
And I cried, "It was surely October,
  On this very night of last year,
  That I journeyed—I journeyed down here—
  That I brought a fair maiden down here,

On this night of all nights in the year.
Ah! to me that inscription is clear;
Well I know now, I'm perfectly sober,
Why no longer they credit me here—
Well I know now that music of Auber
And this Nightingale, kept by one Shear.

NORTH BEACH.

AFTER SPENSER.

LO! where the castle of bold Pfeiffer throws
Its sullen shadow on the rolling tide—
No more the home where joy and wealth repose,
But now where wassailers in cells abide;
See yon long quay that stretches far and wide,
Well known to citizens as wharf of Meiggs;
There each sweet Sabbath walks in maiden pride
The pensive Margaret, and brave Pat, whose legs
Encased in broadcloth oft keep time with Peg's.

Here cometh oft the tender nursery maid,
While in her ear her love his tale doth pour;

Meantime her infant doth her charge evade,
And rambleth sagely on the sandy shore,
Till the sly sea-crab, low in ambush laid,
Seizeth his leg and biteth him full sore.
Ah me! what sounds the shuddering echoes bore,
When his small treble mixed with Ocean's roar.

Hard by, there stands an ancient hostelrie,
And at its side a garden, where the bear,
The stealthy catamount, and coon, agree
To work deceit on all who gather there;
And when Augusta—that unconscious fair—
With nuts and apples plyeth Bruin free,
Lo! the green parrot claweth her back hair,
And the grey monkey grabbeth fruits that she
On her gay bonnet wears, and laugheth loud in glee!

NOTES.

THE LOST GALLEON.—As the custom on which the central incident of this legend is based may not be familiar to all readers, I will repeat here, that it is the habit of navigators to drop a day from their calendar in crossing westerly the 180th degree of Longitude W. of Greenwich, adding a day in coming East, and that the idea of the Lost Galleon had an origin as prosaic as the Log of the first China mail steamer from this port. The explanation of the custom and its astronomical relations belong rather to the usual text books, than poetical narration. If any reader thinks I have overdrawn the credulous superstitions of the ancient navigators, I refer him to the veracious statements of Moldonado, De Fonté, the later voyages of La Perouse and Anson, and the charts of 1640.

In the charts of "that day" Spanish navigators reckoned Longitude East 360 degrees from the meridian of the Isle of Ferro. For the sake of perspicuity before a modern audience, the more recent meridian of Madrid was substituted. The custom of dropping a day at some arbitrary point in crossing the Pacific westerly, I need not say, remains unaffected by any change of meridian.

I know not if any galleon was ever really missing. For 250 years they made an annual trip between Acapulco and Manila. It may be some satisfaction to the more severely practical of my readers to know, that, according to the best statistics of insurance, the loss during that period would be exactly three vessels and six hundredths of a vessel, which would certainly justify me in this summary disposition of *one*.

THE GODDESS.—Contributed to the Fair for the Ladies' Patriotic Fund of the Pacific.

RELIEVING GUARD.—THOMAS STARR KING died March 4th, 1864.

THE PLIOCENE SKULL.—This extraordinary fossil is in the possession of Dr. Whitney, of the State Geological Survey. The poem was based on the following paragraph from the daily press of 1866:

"A HUMAN SKULL has been found in California, in the pliocene formation. This skull is the remnant not only of the earliest pioneer of this State, but the oldest known human being. . . . . . The skull was found in a shaft one hundred and fifty feet deep, two miles from Angel's, in Calaveras County, by a miner named James Matson, who gave it to Mr. Scribner, a merchant, who gave it to Dr. Jones, who sent it to the State Geological Survey. . . . The published volume of the State Survey on the Geology of California states, that man existed here contemporaneously with the mastodon; but this fossil proves that he was here before the mastodon was known to exist."

www.ingramcontent.com/pod-product-compliance
Lightning Source LLC
Chambersburg PA
CBHW020807020726
47495CB00008B/2620